"To my mother, Marion Lyman Carlisle,
who has always sung to her children."

Book design by Lucy Nielsen and Vandy Ritter. Typeset in CG Bernhard
Modern and Papyrus. The illustrations in this book were rendered in pen and ink
with watercolor.

ISBN 0-590-10739-9

12 11 10 9 8 7 6 5 4   9/9 0 1 2/0

Printed in the U.S.A.   23

First Scholastic printing, September 1997

Hush Little Baby

Sylvia Long

A TRUMPET CLUB SPECIAL EDITION

A Note from Sylvia Long

As much as I love being an artist, my favorite and most important profession has been being a mother. I sang and read to my children, just as my mother sang and read to me. One of the songs that has bothered me as an adult is the original version of "Hush Little Baby." In it, a mama offers her baby comfort by promising to buy him or her all sorts of things (a mockingbird, a diamond ring, horse and cart, etc.). It seems much healthier to encourage children to find comfort in the natural things around them and the warmth of a mother's love. This belief was my inspiration for a new version, which I hope you will enjoy as much as I enjoyed creating it.

Sylvia Long

Hush little baby, don't say a word,

Mama's going to show you a hummingbird.

If that hummingbird should fly,
Mama's going to show you the evening sky.

When the nighttime shadows fall,
Mama's going to hear the crickets call.

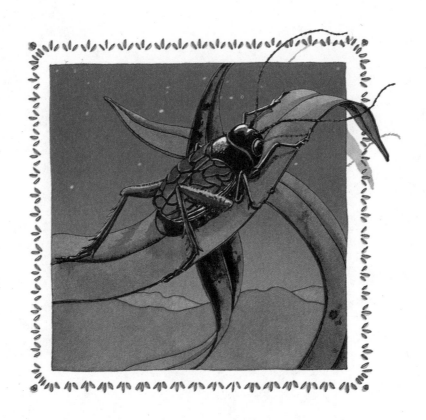

While their song drifts from afar,
Mama's going to search for a shooting star.

When that star has dropped from view,

Mama's going to read a book with you.

When that story has been read,
Mama's going to bring your warm bedspread.

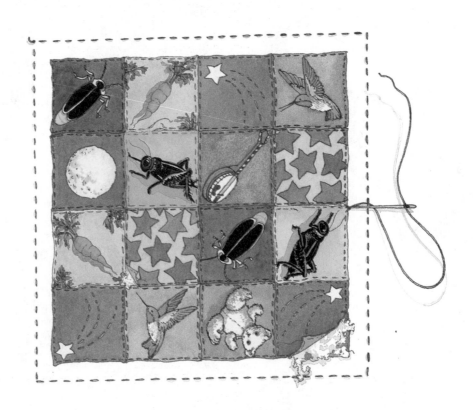

If that quilt begins to wear,

Mama's going to find your teddy bear.

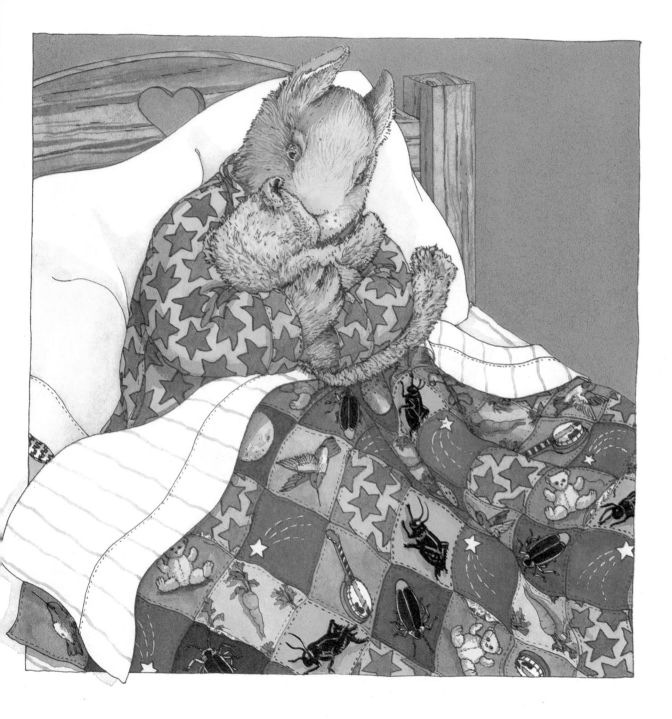

If that teddy bear won't hug,

Mama's going to catch you a lightning bug.

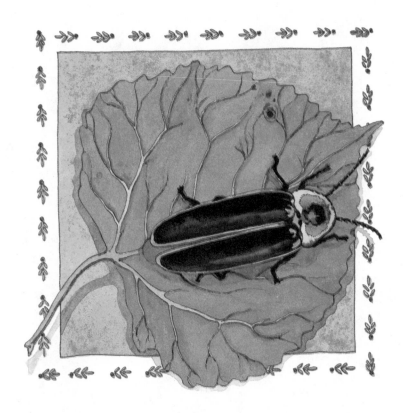

If that lightning bug won't glow,

Mama's going to play on her old banjo.

If that banjo's out of tune,

Mama's going to show you the harvest moon.

As that moon drifts through the sky,
Mama's going to sing you a lullaby.